In honor and memory of Roca,
who inspired and helped me write this book

—Judy

For Libby

—Andrea

Text Copyright © 2011 Judy Young
Illustration Copyright © 2011 Andrea Wesson

Sleeping Bear Press™

315 East Eisenhower Parkway, Suite 200
Ann Arbor, MI 48108
www.sleepingbearpress.com

© 2011 Sleeping Bear Press is an imprint of Gale,
a part of Cengage Learning.

10 9 8 7 6 5 4 3 2 1

Library of Congress Cataloging-in-Publication Data

Young, Judy.
A pet for Miss Wright / written by Judy Young ;
illustrated by Andrea Wesson.
p. cm.
Summary: A lonely writer searches for the perfect pet
to keep her company in her solitary work.
ISBN 978-1-58536-509-8
[1. Pets--Fiction. 2. Authorship--Fiction.] I. Wesson, Andrea, ill. II. Title.
PZ7.Y8664Pe 2011
[E]--dc22
2010034399

Printed by China Translation & Printing Services Limited, Guangdong
Province, China. 1st printing. 12/2010

A Pet for

Written by
Judy Young

Miss Wright

Illustrated by
Andrea Wesson

Miss Wright was an author.

It was a very lonely job. Every day, she sat by herself at her desk and typed. All sorts of exciting things happened in the words that filled the computer screen.

Characters had adventures in exotic places. They talked and laughed with their friends. They narrowly escaped their enemies.

But, except for the click of the keyboard, it was silent in Miss Wright's office.

"It's too quiet," Miss Wright thought.
"I need something to keep me company."

So Miss Wright went to the pet store.

"I have just the thing," said the man in the pet store. He brought out a bird. "Mynahs repeat everything they hear. It will talk to you."

But when Miss Wright took
the bird home, the mynah did not
say any words. It only imitated
the keyboard clicking away in
Miss Wright's quiet office.

Miss Wright took the mynah back and brought home a monkey.

The monkey certainly kept Miss Wright entertained,
but now her stories made no sense.
When Miss Wright typed,
the monkey put his hands on the keyboard, too.
A scramble of mixed-up letters filled the
computer screen.

"Nothing exotic,"
Miss Wright told the man
at the pet store as she
returned the monkey.
"Maybe just a fish."

The fish stared at Miss Wright from
its bowl with its large, goggly eyes.
Miss Wright stared back. Soon they
had hypnotized each other and no words
appeared on the computer screen for days.

Miss Wright thought a hamster might be better.

It ran around and around and around on its wheel. Miss Wright's eyes went around and around and around, too.

She became too dizzy to write and had to lie down to rest.

Next, Miss Wright tried a cat.

It was lazy and liked to lie all day in the sun.
The sun shone through the window across
Miss Wright's desk. The cat stretched out
across the keyboard, quite comfy until dark.

Miss Wright fell asleep
trying to write at night.

"No more pets,"
Miss Wright said.

But when she took the cat back,
the man at the pet store insisted,
"You must try a dog."

Miss Wright did not think a dog would be any better than the other pets. But as she typed, the dog rested quietly on the floor beside her and Miss Wright was not as lonely.

She decided to keep the dog another day. And another. And another.

Every day the dog lay by Miss Wright
as the screen filled with words. When
Miss Wright stopped typing, the dog
sat up, put his head on her desk, and
looked at the computer screen to see
what she had written.

Miss Wright read the words aloud. If the dog
liked the story, he gave her a kiss.

If the dog thought it was sad,
he buried his head in Miss Wright's
lap and whined.

If the dog thought it was funny,
he howled.

But if he didn't like what Miss Wright wrote, he ran and got his leash.

Together, he and Miss Wright would take a long walk so they could think of better ideas.

One day Miss Wright typed the last word of a story.
She printed it off and read it to the dog.

The dog whined at the right places. He howled at the right times.

When Miss Wright finished reading, the dog wagged his tail,
but did not give Miss Wright any kisses.

Miss Wright thought her story was finished. But the dog didn't think so.

The dog chewed a red pencil to a sharp point.
He fetched a thesaurus and a dictionary.

He waited as Miss Wright chose some fancier
words and corrected her spelling mistakes.

Now the story was perfect and the dog
gave Miss Wright lots of kisses.

Miss Wright printed up the revised story
and put it in an envelope.

The dog licked the seal.

He pressed the stamp down with his paw.

SLEEPING BEAR PRESS

Then, with the envelope in his mouth, the dog ran down the driveway to wait for the mailman.

A few weeks later,
the phone rang.
Miss Wright
answered it.

The dog put his head close to the phone so he could hear, too. "It's accepted!" she said to the dog.
"My story will be a book!"

Miss Wright jumped up and down.
                    The dog jumped up and down, too.

                    Miss Wright howled.
                              The dog howled.

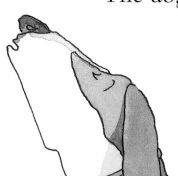

The dog chased his tail. Miss Wright spun around and around in her chair until she fell out.

The dog gave her lots and lots of kisses. Miss Wright gave the dog lots and lots of kisses, too.

Then Miss Wright calmly sat down at her desk again.
The dog lay at her feet as she started typing.

Miss Wright is an author and that's what authors do. It's a lonely job.

Unless you have a dog.